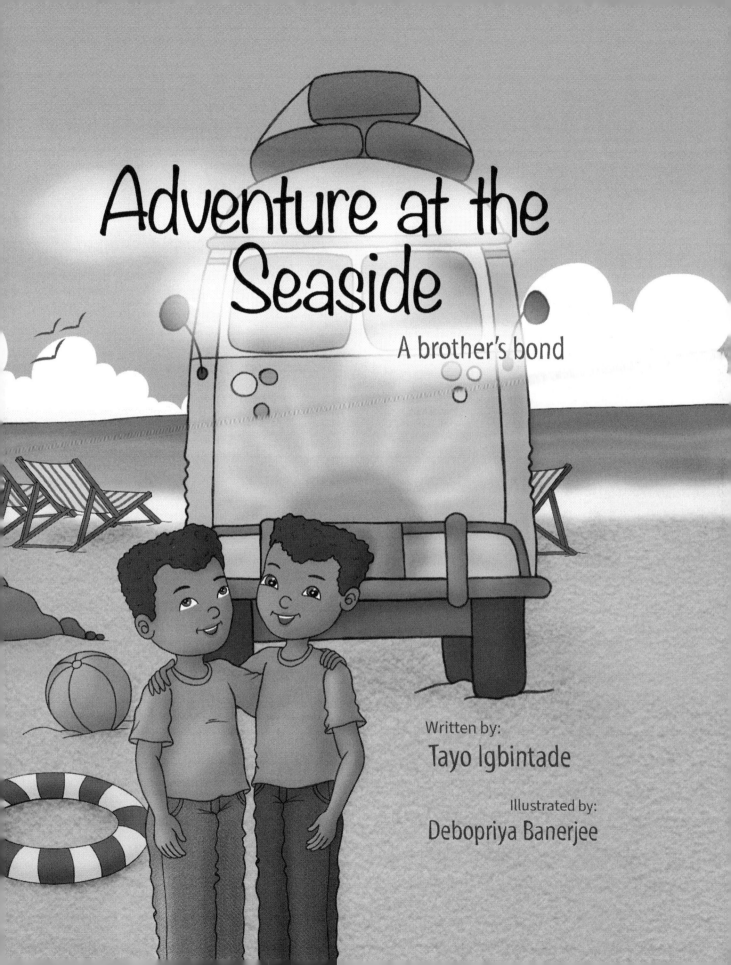

Adventure at the Seaside

A brother's bond

Written by:

Tayo Igbintade

Illustrated by:

Debopriya Banerjee

To David and Jonathan and all siblings of autistic children - this is for you.

My thanks to the members of the PPP and ISL - you know who you are.

Much appreciation to Gemma Bond, for pushing and encouraging me all the way.

Andrew L Ramirez - here's another one for your wall. Thanks for your enthusiasm, energy and mentorship.

This book belongs to

On the day of the trip to the seaside, Jason, Mum, and Joshua ate their breakfast.

Jason had bacon, eggs, and toast.

Mum had some cereal and a cup of tea.

Joshua had the same thing he ate everyday – porridge.

Jason and Joshua were identical twins.

They looked exactly the same with a small difference.

Jason was a tiny bit taller, and Joshua was a little bit bigger.

They had one very big difference, though.

Joshua was autistic.

This meant Joshua needed his clothes to stay clean.

He couldn't stand loud sounds.

Joshua couldn't talk properly, so he used sign language.

He understood when people talked to him, but he couldn't talk back.

And when Joshua was angry, or frustrated or overwhelmed,

he did strange things.

Like rocking backwards and forwards.

Or spinning round and round in circles.

Mum called this stimming when he did that.

When he was really upset, he screamed and hit his face

with both hands.

After breakfast, it was time to go.

Jason was so excited.

"May I carry the buckets and spades? I want to swim with my friends!"

They didn't have to go far to get to the coach.

Jason talked to Mum about all the things they were going to do that day. Joshua listened to soft music on his headphones while he walked.

On the coach, Joshua and Mum sat together.

This trip to the seaside was an unusual outing.

They didn't go out much as a family.

Joshua found it hard to cope with big groups of people.

Jason sat with one of his friends from school called Glenn.

Very soon, the coach was full, and the driver pulled away.

"Let's sing a song," said Glenn.

"I know what song we should sing,"
called out Sade, one of Jason's neighbours.

"Oh, I do like to be beside the seaside," she sang.

Everyone joined in and sang loudly.
They were all happy.
Everyone except Joshua.

Joshua stood up, covered his ears and started rocking back and forth, humming at the same time. Glenn looked back at Joshua.

"I didn't know you had a twin!" he said.

"Why doesn't he go to our school? And what's wrong with him?"

Jason wanted to hide.

Jason hated it when Joshua started his "behaviours" and people talked about his brother like that.

"There's nothing wrong with him!" He tried not to shout.

"He's autistic, so his brain works differently to everyone else.

The singing is too loud for him."

"Oh! Alright. I didn't know," Glenn said. "We can sing quietly."

Glenn could tell that Jason was upset.

So, he turned back to the front and didn't mention Joshua again.

Finally, the coach arrived at the seaside.

They all rushed off the coach, and the children

started to play.

Joshua and Mum found a spot on the beach.

Mum got out a blanket and made herself comfortable.

Jason went toy paddling in the sea with some friends.

At lunchtime, Mum got out their packed lunches from

the picnic basket.

Cheese sandwiches for Jason, and marmalade sandwiches

for Joshua.

They had some crisps, some biscuits, and drinks, too.

After they ate, Jason went back to the sea with his friends.

Joshua really wanted to go with Jason.

Mum wouldn't let him go.

He loved swimming, but Mum was scared that he would

swim out too far and wouldn't be able to get back in safely.

Mum read her book, and checked her phone.
After a little while, Mum realised Joshua was gone.
She looked around, but couldn't find him.

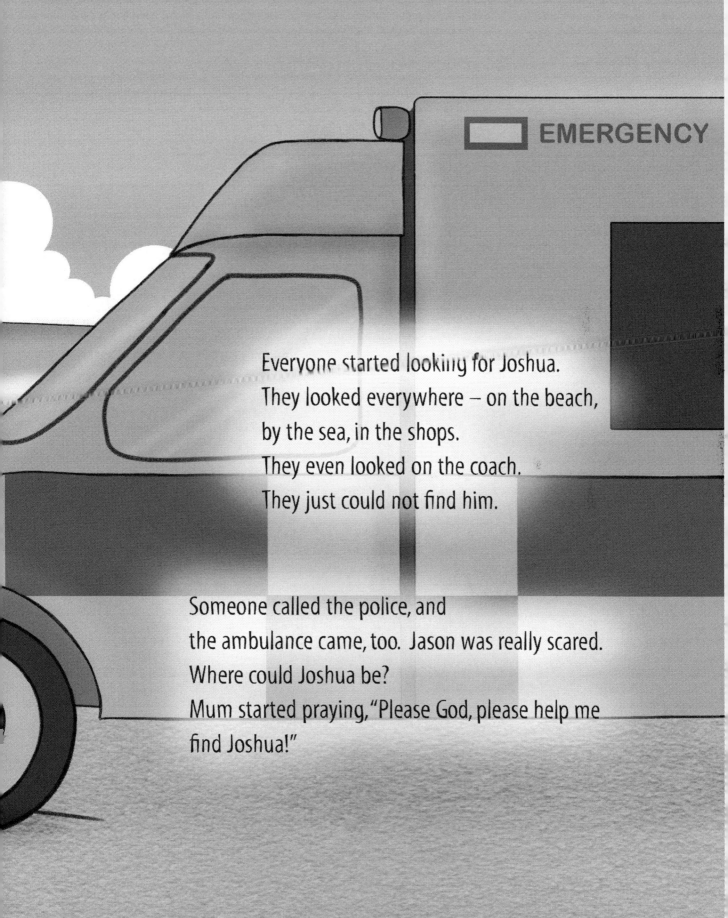

Everyone started looking for Joshua.
They looked everywhere – on the beach,
by the sea, in the shops.
They even looked on the coach.
They just could not find him.

Someone called the police, and
the ambulance came, too. Jason was really scared.
Where could Joshua be?
Mum started praying, "Please God, please help me
find Joshua!"

Suddenly Jason had an idea!
"I know what to do. I'll sing Joshua's favourite song.
You know! The Power Ranger song."
Mum wasn't sure, but maybe the song would help.

"It will definitely work! I know it will," he said confidently.
"Uh Oh, we're in trouble," Jason started singing at the
top of his voice.
Everyone looked at him funny, wondering what on earth
he was doing.

To everyone's surprise, Joshua came running up
to where Jason was singing.

Mum grabbed him and hugged him tight.
Jason high-fived his brother.

To Mum he said, "I told you I'd find him. I knew
he was alright."

Joshua smiled at his brother and said, "happy,"
in sign language.
Everyone was so glad he was safe and sound.

Jason stayed with his brother for the rest of the day.

He played with him, and made sure he was happy and okay.

On the journey back home, Jason sat with Joshua gladly.

On the evening after the trip to the seaside, Jason and Joshua sat at the table while Mum made hot chocolate for them.

"We had quite an adventure today," she said, as she handed them their drinks.

"Definitely a day to remember," said Jason. Joshua nodded in agreement.

"I'm so happy we found you. You're my most favourite brother in the whole wide world, and I love you just the way you are!"

Mum smiled. "That's lovely. Now hurry up my two sleepy heads. It's time for bed."

About the Author

Tayo Igbintade navigated health, education, and social services for 29 years while raising her autistic son and his neurotypical twin. She became a passionate advocate for autistic children and adults during this time. Tayo took this passion to the public arena by supporting a fellow parent, Ivan Corea, in his successful campaign to have 2002 declared Autism Awareness Year in the UK.

She also participated in a steering group for the National Autistic Society in their efforts to better support their first Black and Minority Ethnic group. She continues to work with parents to support their autistic children to thrive and reach their full potential.

Tayo is employed as a British Sign Language/English Interpreter in a range of settings. She is currently training to be a parent advocate to support parents of children with special educational needs. She is an author and speaks on autism related topics, especially about how autism intersects with faith. Her second book, Wonderfully Complex will be published in Spring 2021.

Tayo lives in South London near her twin sons, who share her love of holidays and all things to do with tourism. She loves reading, Star Trek (but not Star Wars), criminal procedurals and cake.

www.tayoigbintade.com